BOYS RULE!

Pie-eating Champions

lice Arena and Phil Kettle

il........ ...d b.

G

R......RS

First Published in Great Britain by
RISING STARS UK LTD 2006
22 Grafton Street, London, W1S 4EX

For more information visit our website at:
www.risingstars-uk.com

British Library Cataloguing in Publication Data
A CIP record for this book is available from the British Library.

ISBN: 978-1-84680-051-1

First published in 2006 by
MACMILLAN EDUCATION AUSTRALIA PTY LTD
627 Chapel Street, South Yarra 3141

Visit our website at www.macmillan.com.au or
go directly to www.macmillanlibrary.com.au

Associated companies and representatives throughout the world.

Series created by Felice Arena and Phil Kettle
Project management by Limelight Press Pty Ltd
Cover and text design by Lore Foye
Illustrations by Gus Gordon

Printed in China

UK Editorial by Westcote Computing Editorial Services

Contents

Billy   Sam

CHAPTER 1

Pie Season

Sam is playing basketball with his friends in the school playground. A few moments later his best friend Billy appears, puffing and holding a newspaper in his hand.

Billy "Didn't you say you've been saving up to buy a PlayStation Portable?"

Sam "Yes, a PSP. Why?"

Billy "Look what's in the school paper. I just grabbed it and sprinted here as fast I could. I was flying!"

Sam "What is it?"

Billy "It's about the school fête."

Billy (reading) "Enter the pie-eating contest this year and win a PlayStation Portable."

Sam "Cool, I wish I had a chance."

Billy "What do you mean?"

Sam "Are you forgetting Hugo Munchen? He's been the pie-eating champion for the past three years in a row."

Billy "So? That doesn't mean he's going to win this year."

Sam "Did you see him at lunch today? He ate a ham and tomato roll the size of a submarine! He's a real mean eating-machine—a pie-eating legend."

Billy "So? That shouldn't stop you from entering! I've heard your Mum say to you a zillion times that you're a bottomless pit!"

Sam "Hmmm ... that's true."

Billy "So what are you? A wimp, or the next pie-eating champion?"

Sam "I suppose I could be a pie-eating champion."

Billy "I didn't hear you. A what?"

Sam (raising his voice) "A pie-eating champion!"

Billy "Say it like you mean it!"

Sam (louder) "*A pie-eating champion!!*"

Billy and Sam's friends all stop and look in their direction.

Billy "You can do better than that!"

Sam "I AM A PIE-EATING CHAMPION!!!!!!!!!!!!!!!!!!!!!!!!!"

Billy "Cool, because I'm going to be your trainer."

CHAPTER 2

No Pain, No Gain

After school Billy goes to Sam's house. They are in the garden and Billy is taking Sam through a pie-eating training course. Billy holds Sam's feet down as he does some sit-ups.

Sam "I don't know why I have to do this. It's got nothing to do with eating pies."

Billy "Because you need strong stomach muscles to stuff as much pie into your tummy as you can! Keep going and don't ask any more questions. Remember, do what your trainer tells you."

Sam "OK, OK, Coach."

Sam does another two sit-ups before
Coach Billy tells him to stand up.

Billy "Right. Now I want you to open
and shut your mouth as fast as you
can. I'm going to use my stopwatch
to see how many times you can do it
in one minute. Ready?"

Sam "Not really."

Billy "Go!"

Sam does as he is told until suddenly he begins to cough and choke.

Billy "What's wrong?"

Sam (coughing) "I think I swallowed a fly! Yuk!"

Billy "That's good. You need to be able to eat stuff you don't like. Remember, there's always the surprise gross pie!"

Sam "The *what* pie?"

Billy "If you make it to the final, they always throw in a surprise gross pie. Just when you get used to eating apple pie with whipped cream, they throw in a broccoli pie with cream instead."

Sam "Yuk! Gross! Puke city!"

Billy "Exactly. That's how Hugo's won every time. He loves eating the surprise gross pies. Everyone else has to stop because they're vomiting. That's how you can beat him. You have to get used to eating stuff you don't like without being sick. Remember, no pain, no gain!"

Sam "I'm not sure if I want to do this now."

Billy "Yes, you do, because what are you?"

Sam *"I'm a pie-eating champion!!"*

Billy "Good. Now follow me. Time for your next exercise."

CHAPTER 3

Don't You Dare!

Sam follows Billy inside.

Sam and Billy are in the kitchen.
Sam is sitting at the kitchen table
with Billy by his side holding a
stopwatch. On the table, in front of
Sam, sits an apple pie with whipped
cream on top.

Sam "I can't believe you bought this pie with your own pocket money."

Billy "Believe it! I want to see you win."

Sam "Why?"

Billy "Because *your* PSP will be *my* PSP."

Sam "Right, as if."

Billy "OK. I'm going to time you to see how long you take to eat the whole lot. Ready? Set. Go!"

Sam gobbles down the pie. He gets cream all over his face as he tries to shove as much pie into his mouth as he can.

Billy "Faster! Faster! 35 seconds! Eat! Eat! Eat!"

Sam (mumbling) "I'm going as fast as I can!"

Billy "Come on, eat faster! 49
 seconds! You've still got heaps to go!"

Sam dips his fingers into the pie and
flicks some whipped cream into Billy's
face. Billy wipes the cream off his face
and smears it on Sam's forehead. Sam
stops eating.

Billy "What are you doing? Keep
 going! You're wasting time!"

Sam holds the pie in his hand, as if he's about to throw it. Billy steps back away from him.

Billy "Don't you dare! I'm your trainer. Put it down!"

Sam gives a wicked grin and steps towards Billy.

Billy "Sam, remember why we're doing this. What are you?"

Sam raises the pie.

Sam *"I'm a pie-eating champion!!"*
Billy "That's right ... so, put the pie down. No, Sam, no!"

But it's too late. Sam flings the pie
at Billy. Billy ducks just in time.
The pie flies over his head and across
the room, just as Sam's father enters
the kitchen. *Splat!*

CHAPTER 4

Spots

It's the following morning—the day of the school fête and the pie-eating contest. Sam and Billy meet each other at the front gates.

Billy "Hey, what happened after your Dad told me to leave?"

Sam "He was really angry with me. He's never had a pie thrown in his face before."

Billy "So what's with the weird spots all over you?"

Sam "It's hives."

Billy "What? Beehives?"

Sam "No. After you left I broke out in hives. They'll be gone by lunchtime, but the doctor reckons I'm allergic to the cream on the pies."

Billy "What? You can't be? What about the contest? You have to still enter the contest."

Sam "I'm not allowed to. Sorry, Coach."

Billy "But all that hard work and training ... oh, man, this isn't fair!"

Sam "Why don't you do it?"

Billy "What?"

Sam "Yes, *you* enter the contest."

Billy "Hmm. Do you think so?"

Sam "Yes. You've got what it takes to be a pie-eating machine. You could be a champion, too."

Billy "Hmm. I do like pies. And I do like eating. And I do want to win a PSP."

Sam "Which you'd share with me."

Billy "Maybe. And it would make me famous. So famous, that I'd be invited to compete at pie-eating contests right around the world. Maybe I could be a pie-eating wrestler Yes, I'd wrestle these big men and my trademark would be that I'd eat a pie after I slammed them to the floor."

Sam "Now you're dreaming."

Billy "All right! I'm going to do it! I'm going to enter the pie-eating contest!"

CHAPTER 5

Pie-eating Champions

The pie-eating contest is on. Billy eats his way through two rounds and then a semi-final. Sam cheers for him all the way. It's nearly time for the final.

Sam "That was amazing! You're in the final."

Billy "I feel like I'm going to explode."

Sam "Well, don't, because this is the big one. You can do it."

Billy "Hugo Munchen's in it as well. Again."

Sam "So what? You ate as many pies as he did in that first round. You've got a good chance. Now get in there and eat some pie!"

The pie-eating finalists are called to take up their positions. Sam is standing at the front of the crowd.

Sam "Go Billy! Eat like an animal!"

The referee blows his whistle and the finalists scoff down their pies.

Sam "Go Billy! Go! Go! Go!"

Suddenly, the finalists are given a surprise gross pie—asparagus and whipped cream. Some competitors begin to be sick, all except for Billy and the pie-eating legend.

Sam "Yes, Billy! Don't look at them. Keep your eyes on the pie! Eat that asparagus. Remember what you said to me—no pain, no gain!"

With only seconds to go, it's clear to everyone that the contest is now between Billy and Hugo.

Sam "Come on, Billy! Don't stop now."

Finally, the referee signals that time is up and announces that Billy has eaten the most pies.

Sam "That was amazing!"

Billy "I was *this* close to throwing up."

Sam "Yes, but you didn't. You did it! You did it!"

Billy "What do you mean *I* did it … *we* did it! Because what are we?"

Sam and Billy "WE'RE PIE-EATING CHAMPIONS!!!!!"

Sam

Billy

BOYS RULE!

Pie-eating Lingo

bucket A plastic tub that a pie-eating contestant has nearby just in case they have to throw up from eating too many pies—yuk!

champion A person who keeps winning the same event (like pie eating).

fête An outdoor festival. The perfect place for a pie-eating contest.

shove When you ram or push something like a pie into your mouth. But remember to chew!

whipped cream Cream that's been beaten until it goes fluffy. Not cream that's been hit with a whip. It's not as violent as it sounds.

BOYS RULE!
Pie-eating Must-dos

☞ Wear a serviette if you want to protect what you're wearing. In a pie-eating contest there's bound to be pie and cream flying everywhere.

☞ Have something to drink nearby to help wash the pie down. Water or chilled milk is the best.

☞ Try not to eat anything for at least an hour before a pie-eating contest. Make sure there's plenty of room in your stomach for all those pies.

☞ Remember to chew. You don't want to choke to death and interrupt the entire competition.

☞ If you find yourself in a messy pie-eating contest that might turn into a pie fight, it's a good idea to wear swimming goggles. You don't want to get cream in your eyes!

☞ Ask if your school can have a pie-eating contest at your next school fête.

☞ You might want to train for your pie-eating contest beforehand. You'll need a friend to be a timekeeper. Ask your mum if she'll let you eat an entire pie one night after dinner.

Pie-eating
Instant Info

The largest custard pie fight ever recorded took place in April 2000. 3,312 pies were thrown by 20 people in three minutes at the London Millennium Dome.

In America, sweet pies like apple pie and custard cream pie are usually more popular than savoury ones. At Thanksgiving, lots of Americans eat pumpkin pie and pecan pie.

Pie-eating contests are sometimes held at school fêtes in Australia and at county fairs in America.

Many comedians use a pie in their performances. Seeing a pie thrown at someone's face is always funny—but not for the one who has pie all over their face.

The meat pie is a popular British dish.

The largest apple pie ever baked was made in 1977 in Washington, USA. The pie dish measured 13.4 metres x 7.3 metres. Now that's a lot of pie!

BOYS RULE!

Think Tank

1 How many pies do you have to eat to be a pie-eating champion?

2 What's in an apple pie?

3 What do you call cream and pie flying all over the place?

4 What buzzes and doesn't taste half as good as a pie?

5 What sound does a pie in the face make?

6 What gets whipped but never gets hurt? Clue: you find it on top of pies.

7 What could you expect to find in a gross pie?

8 Billy is a pie-eating champion. True or false?

Answers

1 You'd have to eat more pies than the other competitors.

2 An apple pie is full of apples, of course!

3 You'd call cream and pie flying all over the place the ultimate pie fight, or a huge mess.

4 A fly buzzes and doesn't taste half as good as a pie. Just ask Sam.

5 Splat! Plosh! Squish! Sploosh! are all acceptable and ... also, "Mmmm, this pie tastes great!".

6 Cream gets whipped, but never gets hurt.

7 You could expect to find asparagus in a gross pie.

8 True. Billy is a pie-eating champion.

How did you score?

- If you got all 8 answers correct, then you have all the makings of a true pie-eating legend.

- If you got 6 answers correct, then you like to eat pies, but at your own pace—while watching someone get a pie in the face.

- If you got fewer than 4 answers correct, then you enjoy eating the occasional pie, but you'd be a better pie-eating trainer rather than a competitor.

Felice → ← Phil

Hi Guys!

We have heaps of fun reading and want you to, too. We both believe that being a good reader is really important and so cool.

Try out our suggestions to help you have fun as you read.

At school, why don't you use "Pie-eating Champions" as a play and you and your friends can be the actors. Set the scene for your play. Bring a stopwatch to school to use as a prop. You might be lucky enough to talk your Mum or Dad into baking a couple of pies to use. Try not to make too much mess!

So ... have you decided who is going to be Billy and who is going to be Sam? Now, with your friends, read and act out our story in front of the class.

We have a lot of fun when we go to schools and read our stories. After we finish the children all clap really loudly. When you've finished your play your classmates will do the same. Just remember to look out the window—there might be a talent scout from a television channel watching you!

Reading at home is really important and a lot of fun as well.

Take our books home and get someone in your family to read them with you. Maybe they can take on a part in the story.

Remember, reading is fun.

So, as the frog in the local pond would say, Read-it!

And remember, Boys Rule!

Phil "Have you ever entered a pie-eating contest?"

Felice "Yes. I'm a pie-eating legend."

Phil "Really?"

Felice "Yes, I love apple pie, apricot pie, lemon pie, pumpkin pie and coconut cream pie."

Phil "That's a lot of pies!"

Felice "But mostly, I love sea pie."

Phil "You mean, like fish pie?"

Felice "No, see pie. Every pie I see, I eat!"

What a Laugh!

Sam

Q What type of pies do Egyptians eat?

A The pies that mummies make.

Billy

BOYS RULE!

 Gone Fishing

 The Tree House

 Golf Legends

 Camping Out

 Bike Daredevils

 Water Rats

 Skateboard Dudes

 Tennis Ace

 Basketball Buddies

 Secret Agent Heroes

 Wet World

 Rock Star

 Pirate Attack

 Olympic Champions

 Race Car Dreamers

 Hit the Beach

 Rotten School Day

 Halloween Gotcha!

 Battle of the Games

 On the Farm

BOYS RULE! books are available from most booksellers.
For mail order information please call Rising Stars
on 0870 40 20 40 8 or visit www.risingstars-uk.com

44

Oh! Oh! Oh! I feel really poorly!

Brian showed them Zebedee's moustache, rescued from the old factory.

What! What?

Magic thoughts can always give Magic gardens everywhere.

I'm in the dark and lonely
It must be all a dream.

You are going to the moon.

I claim this moon for me –
King Buxton...the First.

Luckily,
Dougal had a parachute...

A triumph! All captured.
The dreaded cactus
everywhere. A triumph!

They were all carried orf by some
dashed soldiery...I found the whole
thing distinctly unfresh.

Could I trouble you men to...like
not rattle your chains so much?
I'd like to get a little sleep here.

The sugar was very tempting...

Oh dear,
it must be way past teatime...

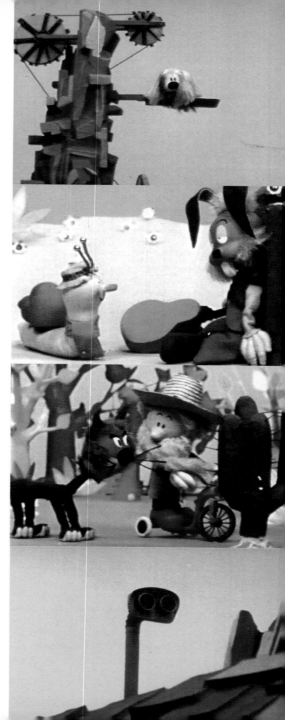

Like...what's wrong, man?

There's been a rash of blue
cactuses...Great prickly
things they are – and blue.

Right, periscope.
Let's look up!

Eee...eck!

I've done it! I've done it!
King Buxton...the First!

We go, we go, we go.

What a lovely example
of my blue period.

I shall sleep like a baby.

Open up! Open up!
I've arrived to claim my rights!

Just a little warning, Buxton.

Frightened, Buxton?

I got myself with some cunning into a position of vantage.

Florence was singing at home...

We've got a beautiful visitor. A blue cat. A beautiful blue cat... called Buxton.

Just a little something. I picked them myself. Sweets to the sweet, you might say.

Now Dougal don't get sloppy!
Just have a cup of tea...

It would be quicker to walk but she
gets very upset...

*Zebedee was conducting a chorus
line of pretty French lollipops.*

I'd gone to bed early with a cup of
cocoa and a biccy.